JACK the WISE and the CORNISH CUCKOOS

by Mary Calhoun
illustrated by Lady McCrady

William Morrow and Company
New York 1978

Library of Congress Cataloging in Publication Data

Calhoun, Mary.
    Jack the Wise and the Cornish cuckoos.

Summary: Jack's reputation for wisdom grows
as he helps the foolish folk of Cornwall.
[1. Folklore—Cornwall.   2. Folklore—England]
I. McCrady, Lady.   II. Title.
PZ8.1.C156Jac   [398.2]   [E]   77-22714
ISBN 0-688-22132-7
ISBN 0-688-32132-1 lib. bdg.

Printed in the United States of America.

First Edition
1 2 3 4 5 6 7 8 9 10

To Gregory the Wise

If you want to know how Jack got his name
and how he helped the foolish folk of Cornwall,
then listen to this tale,
as the old droll tellers would tell it in the chimney corner.

When Jack was a babe,
his godmother Gracey Goosey
came to his naming feast.
She gave him three choices:
a feather,
a currant cake,
and a golden ball.

Jack's little hands picked and pecked
and fastened on the feather.
"Well he has chosen!" cried Gracey Goosey.
"For a cake is soon eaten,
and a ball can roll away,
but a babe can play with a feather for hours.
One day he shall be known as
Jack the Wise."

Then his godmother
summoned her goose,
and they went on their way.
Jack blew on his feather,
and it wafted and tickled
and taught him
to laugh.

He grew up so wise
he always saw the best of things.
When he was hungry, he told himself,
"Food will taste all the better, when it comes."
And so it went.
When Jack's mam and dad died,
he was turned out of the cottage,
and he had no home.
But Jack said to himself,
"Surely, that's for the best,
to have no house.
Now I can travel about
and make new friends."

One night during his wanderings,
a great wind blew a band of sheep
down Gwithian sands and into Saint Ives Bay.
Sheep floated in the water
and were cast up dead on the rocks.
Next day Jack was the first to see
the strange new kind of fish.
"Soas! 'Tis all for the best," he said.
"Cast your nets," Jack called to the fishermen,
"For there's sheep fish afloat in Saint Ives Bay!"

"Heava!" went up the shout
from the fishermen in their boats
and the fishwives with their baskets.
"We'll have 'un!"
With hook and line and webby net,
the men snared the wonderful sheep fish.

Then for ten days 'twas mutton roasted, mutton boiled,
as the fisherfolk made a mutton feast.
And Jack feasted with them.
"Bless Jack!" they cried.
They took up a collection and gave Jack a bag of coins.
Out to Zennor he carried the coins
to order new breeches from Tom the Tailor.

Tom sat cross-legged at his board,
stitching away,
while Jack told how he wanted
his breeches made.
Then through the doorway
came Tom's wife, scolding.
Some called her Dolly Wordy,
for she liked to be right
and have the last word.
"Get up,
you lazy lutterpooch!"
Dolly called to her husband.
"A hundred geese
are trampling down
our field of oats!
Drive them away!"

Tom went to the door.
"What's on your eyes, woman?
I see but two geese in the oats."
"Two!
Why, fifty geese
are destroying our oats."
While Tom and Doll argued,
Jack went out
to drive the geese away.

When he came back, Dolly sat in the corner
with her apron over her head.
"I'll never eat again," she cried,
"until you agree there were at least three geese!"
"Two geese!" Tom called from the table.
"Come, Jack, let's eat."

Jack stayed the night to see things right.
But Dolly Wordy refused to sleep
in her high-standing bed.
"Three geese?"
she called from her pallet on the floor.
"Two geese!"
Tom said from the bed.
In the morning Dolly moaned,
"I'll die of your cruelty.
Send for my mother and sisters,
that I may tell them good-bye.
Or will you admit three geese?"
"Two geese!" Tom shouted.
He flung out of the house, followed by Jack.
"Oh, what shall I do with this stubborn woman?"
Jack laughed.
"Send for a coffin, too," he advised the tailor.
"When Doll sees the box,
she'll know how foolish she's been."
But when they brought the coffin,
Dolly climbed into it.
"For I'm nearly dead," she said.

Lying in the coffin,
she made her sad good-byes
to her mother and sisters,
and the neighbor women came in
to dress the "corpse."
They put a clean cap on her head
and a frill around her face.

A little girl shook flour on Dolly's face,
because she didn't look pale enough.
Tom stormed at Jack.
"You're not so wise! She won't get up!"
"Go on with it," Jack whispered.
"All will happen for the best."
So the neighbors prepared the funeral food
and lit the candles
and watched by the coffin through the night.
They talked about Dolly as if she were dead.
"My, doesn't the corpse look well?"
But she never opened her eyes or her mouth.

In the morning
the neighbors carried the coffin to the graveyard.
As the men dug the hole, Tom knelt by the coffin.
"Please, Doll, stop this foolishness
and get up!" he begged.
"Were the three geese there?"
her voice came faintly.
Tom slung his hat across the churchyard.
"Two geese!" he said.
"I've breathed my last breath!" she said.

Wisely Jack saw
the stubborn woman
would go to her grave
before she'd give in.
So changing his tune, Jack said,
"Wait, I remember!
Through the window
I saw three geese,
but one flew over the house
before Tom got to the door."

"You see?" cried Dolly,
clambering out of the coffin.
"Bless Jack!" cried husband and wife,
as they fell into each other's arms.
"All has happened for the best!"
Hungry Dolly
led everyone back to the house
to eat the funeral feast,
all but Jack.
A runner had come to say
he was needed in Towednack.

of to dwell
in the
Mansions
of Light

She is
Risen
from the
dead

Jack walked up the hills to Towednack Inn,
and who should be the innkeeper
but his godmother, Gracey Goosey.
There sat the men of the village,
puzzling their heads at two problems.
"Here's the wise man we need!"
Gracey Goosey declared.
"Tell Jack the trouble."
First, the miller said, they were tired
of the long, cold winters up there in the hills.
'Twas the last week in April,
and spring had come
to every part of West Cornwall but Towednack.
Second, a farmer told, the people grieved
because they had no yearly festival,
as did the folk of Saint Ives and Saint Buryan.
Their church was only Towednack Church,
with no patron saint
to celebrate with a feasten week,
never a time for merrymaking.
"How can we shorten winter?" the men asked Jack.
"How can we gain a feasten week?"
Jack laughed.
"Soas, all will turn out for the best.
Here's plenty to eat and drink while we think."

So they ate and drank
and thought and talked for days.
Everyone had a fine time at Gracey Goosey's inn,
but no one could think how to shorten winter
or how to gain a feasten week.

"In parts of Cornwall
summer comes at the call of the cuckoo bird,"
said a tin miner.
"The trouble is,
the cuckoo seldom flies to these hills."
"Aha!" cried Jack.
"Next time the cuckoo comes, we'll keep her!
Then we shall have summer as soon as we like.
Let's hedge in a cuckoo!"
"Aye!" shouted the men.
"We'll fence in a cuckoo!"

Out of the inn they streamed and up on a hill.
There they heaved rocks and built a stone wall
around part of the field,
to make a cage for the cuckoo.

"Leave a gap in the wall,
where we'll drive the bird in," said Jack.
He sang, "The cuckoo is a pretty bird,"
and the others joined in,
"And brings us fine weather!"
When the stone hedge was raised,
the men were warm as summer
and merry as a feasten week.
"I see it!" cried Jack.
"'Tis the week of the cuckoo feast!
Tomorrow we'll call in the cuckoo."

Next day was the feasten Sunday.
While the church bells rang in the squatty tower,
all the people met near the inn and formed a procession,
farmers and tin miners, goodwives and children.
The fiddler scraped out a lively tune
and the fifers tweetled,
and they led the folk in a merry prance
to the church door.
After the service, they followed the fiddler
and trooped three times around the village, singing,
"The cuckoo is a pretty bird!"
Then, at tables set outside the inn,
they ate and drank
and sang again.

They named Jack
the king of the Cuckoo Feast,
and Gracey Goosey's prediction came true.
For the people shouted,
"Hurrah for Jack the Wise!"
"Soas!" Jack laughed.
"All has turned out for the best."

No one knows whether the cuckoo bird
ever flew into her stone-hedged field,
crying "Cuck-coo," or how long she stayed.
But the people came to be called
the Towednack Cuckoos.
Every year the good folk held their Cuckoo Feast
the last week of April
and invited their friends from other parishes.
Thus, winter seemed shorter to them ever after.

And every year Jack the Wise
came to join in the merrymaking.
For surely, the wisest of them all
was the leader
of the Towednack Cuckoos!

Author's Notes

In this book I have woven together fragments of folklore found in the nineteenth-century collections of *Traditions and Hearthside Stories of West Cornwall* by Mr. William Bottrell. However, Jack the Wise is a character of my own creation.

Nicknames were common in West Cornwall two centuries ago, for there were many a Tom and Jack and Dolly of the same surname. Thus, one Dolly Trevail might be known as Dolly Winkey and another as Dolly Dancey.... *Soas* is a Cornish word for *forsooth*.... "Heava" was shouted when fish were sighted. The word may be a contraction of "we have them," or, "here they are...." The lines "mutton roasted, mutton boiled," are from a long poem commemorating the Saint Ives mutton feast, written by Mr. Fortescue Hitchins about 1800.... Although the "Three Geese" tale was collected in West Cornwall, it was thought to have traveled there from Ireland.... "Fencing the Cuckoo" is a motif found in various parts of Britain, but the details given here are part of Towednack legend. (Pronounced To*wed*nack.)